Come, Meet Jesus, The Baby

The Story of Matthew 1 and Luke 1—2:20

Kitty Anna Griffiths

Illustrated by "Willy"

ZONDERVAN
PUBLISHING HOUSE
OF THE ZONDERVAN CORPORATION | GRAND RAPIDS, MICHIGAN 49506

Other books in the COME, MEET series:

Adam and Eve
Noah
Abraham, the Pioneer
Abraham, God's Friend
Isaac
Jacob, the Grabbing Twin
Jacob, God's Prince
Joseph, God's Dreamer
Joseph, the Grand Vizier
Ruth
Jesus, the Baby
Jesus, the Boy

All the above books are on cassette, as are many other stories, all told by the author with music and sound effects. They are obtainable from "A Visit With Mrs. G.," Box 179, Station J, Toronto, Ontario, Canada.

COME, MEET JESUS, THE BABY

© 1976 by Kitty Anna Griffiths

First Zondervan edition — 1978

Library of Congress Cataloging in Publication Data

Griffiths, Kitty Anna.
     Come, meet Jesus, the baby.

     (Come, meet series)
     SUMMARY: Relates the events surrounding Jesus' birth including the genealogy of Joseph, the angels' announcements to Elizabeth and to Mary, the births of John the Baptist and of Jesus, and the visit of the shepherds to the stable in Bethlehem.
     1. Jesus Christ—Nativity—Juvenile literature.   2. Bible stories, English—N.T. Gospels.   3. Christian biography—Palestine—Juvenile literature.   [1. Jesus Christ—Nativity.   2. Bible Stories—N.T.]   I. Title.
     BT315.2.G74   232.9'21   78-16703
ISBN 0-310-25241-5

Printed in the United States of America

To my mother,

Annie Grey Arnot Coe

I MUST SAY THANK YOU

to my daughter, Myfanwy Bentley-Taylor, for making me tell her stories when she was little (with her two brothers) and now for helping me to get them ready for you to read. With a doctorate in English Literature, she knows a bit about this sort of thing! I call her my editor.

And to my husband, the Rev. Gerald B. Griffiths, who helps me in every way. He knows so much about the Bible. And I call him my encourager.

And to the government of Israel, who invited me to visit Israel as their guest to see the very places where the Bible stories happened. I'll never forget walking in Nazareth, in Jerusalem, and the thrill of standing in Bethlehem near the spot where the baby Jesus was laid in the manger. There were still sheep and shepherds in the fields nearby.

And thank you, my good friends, my radio listeners of all ages all over the world, who've written to tell me that you loved this Christmas story on radio. "Can we have it written down?" you asked. Here it is in a book illustrated by my friend "Willy," who has made the pages come alive. My grateful thanks to "Willy."

And thank you, God, for Your unspeakable gift—the Baby!

Contents

Preface

All the stories in the COME, MEET series have been leading up to this one, the first of the stories about Jesus. For the birth of Jesus was the fulfillment of a promise, a promise made by God way back in the Garden of Eden at the beginning of time and repeated down the years to chosen men like Abraham.

When Adam and Eve listened to Satan and disobeyed God right at the beginning, God was sad. Sin had crept in to spoil His beautiful world, and the happy relationship between God and man was broken. Adam and Eve had to leave the garden and could only approach God through sacrifices. But God in His love had a great rescue plan to bring man back to Himself. When He banished Adam and Eve from the Garden, God promised that one day, in the future—"in the fullness of time" as the Bible says—He would send His Son, Jesus. He would be the final, all-sufficient sacrifice to close the rift between God and man forever.

This is the story of how God did it—the wonderful story of the first Christmas—the story of the Baby born in a stable, God's secret which He revealed only to a chosen few. It is utterly captivating. Sights, sounds, and smells arise magically before us. Conflicting emotions stir us. We feel we are there, too, participating in the drama.

Mrs. G. invites you to *Come, Meet Jesus, the Baby.*

WHEN JESUS WAS BORN

ISRAEL

GREAT SEA
MEDITERRANEAN

NAZARETH
WHERE THE ANGEL
GABRIEL APPEARED
TO MARY

SAMARIA

TO
EGYPT

BETHLEHEM
WHERE JESUS
WAS BORN

JERUSALEM
WHERE SIMEON
SAW THE
BABY JESUS

SALT
SEA

1

The Promise

God knew exactly what He  would do. He knew exactly.

Satan thought he'd outwitted God when he got Eve to listen to him and disobey God in the Garden of Eden.

"I've ruined His world and His beautiful people. It's all spoiled," Satan gloated. "I hate Him! I hate Him! *I hate Him!*" Satan hissed. "Ah! What will God say? What will God do?" Satan wondered.

Satan certainly underestimated God.

Do you know that before Adam and Eve even got the fig leaves sewed together to make aprons to cover their bodies, God had *the plan* all ready? There'd been a planning meeting in heaven before God came down to speak to Adam and Eve in the garden that evening:

a Savior was to come
who would defeat Satan.
(God said to Eve,
you remember:
"Someone born of
a woman will bruise
the serpent's head"—
Satan's head.)

At the planning
meeting in heaven,
God's only Son, the Lord Jesus,
had volunteered to be the Savior of the world. But to do
it, He would have to lay aside all His power and glory—
for the time being—and become a helpless little baby.
And He would come to earth in the fullness of time. That
just means at the right time— God's time.

The Bible tells us that when the right time came, the
time that God had decided on, He sent His Son, born of
a woman, born as a Jew. The Savior was born in this
way to bring us into God's family, so that we can call
God our dear Father. And since we are God's children,
everything He has belongs to us, for that is the way He
planned it. Isn't that exciting?

You and I are in God's wonderful plan if we have the
Spirit of His Son in our hearts.

And God's wonderful plan was ready then, way back
at the beginning—even before the beginning—
because, being God, God knew what was going to
happen.

The plan was going to take time to work out. But God is never in a hurry, for what He plans is as good as done. God's not the changing kind. So the plan unfolds, bit by bit, like a flower.

After the first promise of the Savior to Adam and Eve in their awful plight, God chose individuals down through the Old Testament to help with the plan. He chose people He could trust and people who trusted Him. Not just clever or cunning people, but faithful, respectful people, trustworthy people. And they all ran their stint in the relay race till the goal was reached.

There was Abraham. "Abraham," God said, "the Savior will be one of your descendants."

Abraham's people became many: there were Isaac, and Jacob, and his twelve sons, the fathers of the Jewish people, and the tribes of Israel. And God said, "The Savior will come from the tribe of Judah."

Centuries went by. David became king, and God said, "The Savior will come from David's line, from the family of King David, and His kingdom will never end."

"He will be born in Bethlehem," God promised. "And His mother will be a virgin."

And the Jewish people longed for Him and looked for Him, their Deliverer. Ah, He'd be a mighty king! He'd lead them against their enemies. Their day was coming.

But at the time our story begins, things were dreadful in Israel, really dreadful. The nation was under the heel of the Roman Empire. Caesar was the emperor who ruled over the whole Roman Empire, but he had kings under him who were in charge of the countries he'd conquered—like Israel.

Herod was king in Israel. Israel hadn't chosen him. He'd been appointed by Rome. He'd ruled Israel for thirty-five years, and he was still at it. But what a horror of a man! He was simply terrified that someone would snatch his throne from under him. He became obsessed with this notion. He was Herod *the Great,* and no mistake about it. He was *the Greatest.* He just had to be. No rivals! Anyone who looked as if he could possibly be a rival lost his head.

This kind of terror—terror of losing his throne—made Herod insane, mad. Herod killed his near and dear in case any of them had an eye on his throne. His favorite wife, Mariamne, had to go. She and her two sons were slain. (Herod actually married ten times.)

He was so cruel that Caesar Augustus said it was safer to be Herod's pig than Herod's son. That was a rather rude national joke.

Herod claimed to be Jewish. He was only half Jewish, but he offered sacrifices every day. His allegiance was to Rome, but he was always afraid the Jewish people would revolt and throw him off his throne. So at times he tried to please them. He knew they thought a lot of their temple at Jerusalem, which needed repairing and rebuilding. So what did he do? He hired ten thousand men to do the job.

The temple pillars, the turrets, the walls gleamed in the sunshine. A great cluster of solid gold grapes, four stories high, decorated the side of the white temple wall. Beautiful!

Sacrifices were offered daily in the temple—morning, noon, and night. But there had been no message from God for four hundred years. No prophet had come. Worship for most people had become formal and remote.

But there were a few faithful people who still watched and waited for the Messiah, the Savior, and they taught their children to do the same, year after year.

Now just at this time when Herod was king, God said, "*Now is the time!* Now is the time for the Savior to be born."

God was well aware of the state of things in the world in general, and in Israel in particular, and He'd picked out His people, His special servants: a lovely devout girl, Mary, to be the Savior's mother; a good kind man,

willy

Joseph, who would one day marry her; and a saintly priest and his wife, Zechariah and Elizabeth, to be the parents of the Savior's herald. There were others too, but these were the four main ones. And they would be specially tested.

"Gabriel!" God said to one of His angels. "I have two errands for you on earth! Take a message to priest Zechariah in Jerusalem, and a message to Mary in Nazareth. Take Zechariah his message now. He's serving in the temple in Jerusalem right now. It's his special duty."

And Gabriel was off to earth.

2

My Wife Is Too Old!

Zechariah and his wife, Elizabeth, were old. They were good people; they kept God's laws carefully. But ever since they'd been married they'd asked God for a baby or two—one to start with!—and no baby had ever arrived.

Zechariah was a priest. And in his priestly prayers he had slipped in his prayer for a baby. So had his wife, Elizabeth: "O God, please send me a baby." The years went by. Prayers for other people were answered, but Elizabeth's prayer for a baby, Zechariah's prayer for a baby—no. Time passed. Many years passed, and still no baby for Elizabeth and Zechariah.

By this time, Elizabeth's hair was white and her face was wrinkled, though beautiful and calm—a little sad perhaps. "I do wish God had sent me a baby," she sighed.

Then one day Zechariah announced to his wife that he had to go to Jerusalem to do temple duty again for a week. All of Zechariah's division of priests would have to do duty on this week. They were like a team.

Lots were cast each morning to determine which priest should do what. Some duties

were more like chores than others, but nobody grumbled so long as the duty fell to each by lot.

At daybreak the first set of lots was cast, and the priests scattered to their tasks: one group cleared out the ashes from yesterday's sacrifice, scrubbed down the altar, and laid fresh wood upon it; another group cleaned the brass candlestick and the altar of incense and prepared the morning sacrifice. The great temple court had to be swept too. Oh, there were a hundred-and-one things to be done!

Soon after the second lot was cast, the great temple doors swung open and three priests blew blasts on their silver trumpets to announce that the morning sacrifice was about to be offered. People began to pour into the temple courts for worship.

Now the third lot was cast, and what do you think? Zechariah was the priest chosen to go into the Holy Place to burn the incense before the Lord and to come out afterwards to bless all the people! Only once in a lifetime did this honor come to a priest. And at last it was Zechariah's turn!

Zechariah was soon to go into the Holy Place—all by himself. Had his wife, Elizabeth, whispered in his ear, "If you're in the Holy Place, all by yourself with God, don't forget to ask about the baby"? I don't know. They were so old, Zechariah and Elizabeth. Maybe they thought they were far too old by now to have a baby.

The silver trumpets sounded again from the temple tower. Time to worship. The sacrifice was offered, and now the priest Zechariah moved into the Holy Place to burn incense before Jehovah.

A great hush fell on the crowd. Would the priest be all right in there? The Scripture said that the priest was not to tarry in the Holy Place any longer than absolutely necessary, so as not to worry the people waiting and worshiping outside. While the incense burned, the people outside prayed and worshiped. When the priest came out again, a gentle relieved sigh would go up from the waiting people. They'd know then that they were accepted, that God had forgiven their sins—if the priest came out again safe.

Zechariah was there, in the Holy Place, burning incense. Moments passed. Minutes passed. . . . Zechariah didn't come out. The crowd became uneasy. They dared not speak; dread came upon them.

What was happening to Zechariah? Inside the Holy Place he stood burning the incense on the golden altar, when suddenly an angel appeared, standing right beside the altar. Zechariah was startled, terrified.

"Don't be afraid," the angel said. "I have come to tell you that your prayer is answered. God has heard it. Your wife, Elizabeth, will have a son. This will give you both great joy and gladness. You are to call him John. He will prepare the way for Messiah. Messiah is coming soon."

Zechariah said, "How ever can this happen to me? I'm old. My wife is old too. It's impossible. I need a sign."

The angel said, "I am Gabriel. I have come from the very presence of God to bring you this message of good news, and you just don't believe me. A sign you'll have, though. Until the baby is born, you won't be able to speak a word. You will be dumb. My words will certainly come true."

Well, Zechariah was dumbstruck, sure enough. And the angel Gabriel went on his way.

The eyes of all the people were fixed on the beautiful drape that hung over the entrance into the Holy Place.

It was a lovely piece of work, that drape. Every known flower was embroidered on it and many fruits, all in gorgeous colors. But their eyes weren't admiring the drape. They were anxious eyes. Their priest had been in there such a long time.

Eventually the drape moved, and Zechariah emerged from the Holy Place. The crowd sighed with relief when they saw him. But he couldn't utter one word of blessing. He had to use gestures to bless the crowd in front of him. The people were very impressed with this, though. They knew he had seen a vision.

Zechariah stayed on in Jerusalem at the temple until his duties were finished. Then he went home again.

He had great news for Elizabeth, his wife, but he wouldn't be able to tell her! He couldn't speak? Would he write her a note? We shall hear what happened.

3

God Chooses Mary

Now God said to Gabriel, His splendid angel messenger: "Gabriel, now is the time for you to take my message to Mary in Nazareth."

Gabriel left and was on his way to earth immediately.

Mary was a beautiful, graceful young lady. All her life she had lived in Nazareth. She'd been born in Nazareth. Her parents weren't rich by any means, but they'd given her something else of great value.

Mary was well-versed in the Scriptures. If anyone remarked on her knowledge of the Scriptures, she'd say, "Well, how can I help knowing them, with parents like mine? I hear them talk. And when Aunt Elizabeth and Uncle Zechariah come to visit, you should hear the conversation then. They quote Scripture by the mile. Uncle Zechariah is a priest, you know. I just love the stories in the Scriptures. I can't help remembering them."

Mary had had some formal education. She didn't have as much schooling as she'd have had if she'd been a boy, but she'd learned her alphabet by drawing the letters on a board till she was really sure of them. She'd had to read aloud so that her diction and pronunciation could be corrected and polished. Children in Israel were treated rather reverently, which was nice! Mary had learned domestic arts:

how to care for a family, how to look after a new baby. She had also trained her memory: teachers insisted that her memory work was to be word-for-word perfect.

And studying nature had taught Mary to be observant. When girls got married and had children, they were expected to teach their children many things before school days ever began.

WILLY

Just lately Mary had become engaged to be married to a kind young man in Nazareth, a carpenter named Joseph.

"You could really trust your life to Joseph," Mary told her mother as they tidied up the house one day. "I like the way he talks of God. Joseph makes me feel safe.

"We won't be rich for sure, but I'm not used to riches. Daddy isn't rich. If Joseph stays well and can work,

we won't starve. He's making our furniture in his shop—his father's shop. By the time we're married, he'll have his own shop. He's making our furniture—the table, the bed, the cupboard for our clothes, and the chest. We'll sit on the floor on rugs, and we'll have to have a little donkey. Oh, yes, there'll be an oven for me to bake the bread. We'll have everything we need."

"To think that this time next year you'll be married, Mary. I shall miss you when you leave home."

"We won't be far away, mother—Joseph's fixing up our little place now. His shop will be right next to our little house. He's so clever with his saw and hammer and nails. I shall be excited when you and daddy visit us with the children."

"You're only the eldest of the children yourself, Mary! Oh, dear, how quickly you all grow up! Well, I must get a few things from the market this morning. You'll find plenty to do while I'm out, Mary. Keep an eye on the bread for me, please. It may be done before I get back. We don't want it overdone." And mother was off down the street.

Mary took a look at the bread in the earthen stone-lined oven. It had a little while to go before being done. So Mary closed the oven door again and turned back towards the table.

There stood a shining angel! It was Gabriel! Mary was startled. She took a step backward.

"Shalom!" said the angel. "And congratulations! Rejoice! You are a favored lady. The Lord is with you!"

willy

26

Mary looked confused and puzzled. What could the angel mean by those words? Now Mary wasn't as frightened as she might have been if she hadn't read about angels in the Scriptures. But still she was frightened.

"Don't be frightened, Mary," the angel said in a kind, reassuring voice. "God has decided to bless you far beyond any other woman. God has chosen you to be the mother of the promised Savior, the Messiah. You will have a baby boy, and you are to call His name Jesus. He will be great. 'The Son of the Most High God' will be His title, and the Lord God will give Him the throne of His ancestor David. He shall reign over Israel for ever. And His kingdom shall never end."

Mary was speechless. She just couldn't take in the message. She—*she* was to be the mother of the Son of God? Wonderful news! Wonderful news about Messiah coming, but—but—

"Oh—please," she said in a quaking voice, and her hands trembled, "—please pardon me, but I must ask you—how ever can this happen to me? I'm not even married, only engaged to be married—how ever can I have a baby? A baby has to have a father, doesn't he?"

The angel gave Mary the kindest smile and explained. "The Holy Spirit will come upon you," he said, "and the power of the Most High will overshadow you. So the baby you will have will be utterly holy—the Son of God. You see?"

Before the angel left, he talked with Mary a little longer, as if to encourage her a bit. He gave Mary some interesting news about her Aunt Elizabeth.

"Your relative Elizabeth, although she is so old, is

going to have a little son in three months' time," Gabriel said. "Nothing is impossible with God," he added.

Those words seemed to give Mary courage. And she said, "I belong to the Lord, body and soul. I am willing to do whatever He wants. May all that you've said to me come true."

In a moment the angel was gone. And Mary stood there in the house alone.

What news! Messiah was coming! And she, Mary, was to be His mother. Mary was so excited she didn't know what to do. Oh, how glad everybody would be that Messiah was coming! Ever since Mary was a little girl she'd heard of Messiah's coming. Scripture said He would come. Her parents, Joseph's parents, Joseph, and others—as well as herself—looked forward to Messiah's coming. Aunt Elizabeth and Uncle Zechariah, the priest,

looked forward to Messiah, to the Savior's coming. Now He was going to come, and she, Mary, was going to be His mother.

"Fancy God choosing me! I'm just a humble girl. Oh, I must tell my mother!"

But as she started off to look for her mother, Mary stopped in her tracks. Mother had waited for Messiah. It would be a great honor for someone to be His mother, but what—what would she say when she knew it was *her* Mary? What would father say? What would Joseph say—oh, what *would* Joseph say . . . ?

Would they believe that an angel had visited her?

Mary's joy and gladness vanished. All she could see was misunderstanding . . . gossip about her in Nazareth . . . and her parents hanging their heads in shame . . . and Joseph, her fiancé, being the butt of ridicule because of her. There could be real trouble with Joseph.

Mary's joy was already turning to bitterness.

No, she couldn't tell her mother. "Maybe God will tell them. Maybe He will." There was no one to whom she could tell her wonderful secret. No one would understand.

Then she remembered the angel's news about Aunt Elizabeth. She'd forgotten about Aunt Elizabeth's news for the moment.

"Why did the angel tell me about Aunt Elizabeth?" she wondered. "Oh, I'd love to see Aunt Elizabeth. I could tell her. She'd understand. She really is very close to God, and Uncle Zechariah is a priest. Yes, they'd understand, and they'd be pleased at my news.

Oh, why does the most wonderful news in all the world have to be a secret just because no one would understand?"

When her mother came in, Mary said, "Mother, I'd really like to go to see Aunt Elizabeth at Ein Karen."

"What?" her mother exclaimed. "In the middle of your engagement year? Mary, what ever next? What will people think of you for doing that? What ever would Joseph say to that?"

"I'd really like to go, mother, if you don't mind. I'm very fond of auntie, you know."

"Well—well—I suppose it will be your last chance to see her before you're married. We'll speak to your father about it."

"Mary wants to go and visit Elizabeth," her father was told. "It's rather nice that she wants to go see our sister, I suppose. Elizabeth's awfully fond of our Mary. What do you think?"

"Well, she certainly can't travel alone. Ein Karen is ninety miles away. We'll have to see if we can find a family traveling south that she can go with, if her mind's set on going. I'd much rather she stayed at home."

But next day Mary's father came in from the market with some news that pleased his daughter. Menfolk usually got their news from the marketplace; women picked up news along with their water pots at the well. Father's news was that he'd heard of a family who would be traveling south in a couple of days' time, and he'd already asked if Mary might travel with them. They were most agreeable. In fact, they welcomed the idea. They had some children, and they'd be nice company for Mary, if she was still bent on going.

Mary was bent on going all right. Aunt Elizabeth was the one person in all the world Mary wanted to see just now. "Thank you, daddy," she said. And she packed her bags, really excited.

The family Mary traveled south with were kind people. They had their own things to think and talk about among themselves. Mary had so much on her mind. Sometimes she was in a daydream of joy as her feet walked along the dusty road. Sometimes she talked with the children and comforted them when they were wearied by the journey. They picked the wayside flowers as they traveled, told each other stories, listened for the different bird songs.

And eventually, they arrived at the home of her aunt and uncle, Elizabeth and Zechariah.

Mary said good-by to her fellow travelers, who had farther to go. She kissed the children and patted the donkeys good-by. Everyone, herself included, was hot and sticky and tired from the journey. Their clothes were dusty, and they longed for cool water to wash their feet.

Left alone to make her way to the house, Mary's heart sank. After all, could she tell *anyone* her secret? Perhaps, after all, she couldn't.

4

Aunt Elizabeth Knew!

"Aunt Elizabeth is the one person in all the world I want to see. I can talk to her. She's always got time to listen, and I can tell her my secret. She'll understand." If Mary had said this to herself once, she'd said it a hundred times. And she'd traveled all the way from Nazareth just to see her aunt. But now as she walked up the pathway to her aunt's house, Mary felt shy.

This was the moment she'd longed for—to arrive at Aunt Elizabeth's house. And now, after all—"Oh, auntie doesn't even know I'm coming. And can I really tell anybody my secret?" Natural misgivings, when she had something as big as that on her mind.

But Mary's courage returned before she reached the house. Happy memories of her aunt's love and kindness encouraged her. Mary's usual bright self took over, and with a light step she reached the doorway.

The stones outside the house were washed down, and the whole place looked beautifully cared for. Flowers were blooming in the garden. Auntie's house was always inviting.

Mary pulled aside the embroidered drape that hung across the doorway and called out: "Aunt Elizabeth! Auntie! I just had to come to see you!"

"That's Mary's voice, surely—Oh, Mary, it's you," a voice called from an inside room. And in no time, Aunt Elizabeth had come out and thrown her outstretched arms around Mary. As kind Aunt Elizabeth kissed her, Mary felt so safe.

"Auntie must have been expecting me," Mary told herself.

Aunt Elizabeth's face did look beautiful. The sad lines were all gone. Her white hair shone, and her smile was absolutely radiant.

"Oh, Mary," she said, "God has favored you above all other women. And your child is destined for God's highest praise. How honored I am that the mother of my Lord should come to visit me! Even my little unborn baby jumped for joy when you came in and greeted me."

So the angel had been right about Aunt Elizabeth's baby. Of course! Mary's courage was growing.

"Mary, you believed what God said would come to pass," Aunt Elizabeth went on. "God could trust you to believe Him. That's why He's given you this wonderful blessing."

Aunt Elizabeth knew! God had told her the secret too. So Mary wouldn't have to tell, and explain, and explain, and convince. Aunt Elizabeth knew! And only God could have told her.

Mary's joy knew no bounds. Oh, she was happy. The whole house felt filled with God's presence. A priest's house should be, of course, but this—oh, this was wonderful. Aunt Elizabeth was certainly filled with God's Holy Spirit.

Mary's doubts, if she had any—certainly her fears—were all gone. She felt at peace, elated, inspired. And she spoke her real feelings right from her heart in a beautiful song which you can read in the Bible. We call it *The Magnificat*.

Elizabeth was thrilled as she listened to Mary's song. Mary's thoughts were expressed in phrases that she'd learned from the Scriptures and stored up in her heart and mind since her childhood days.

When she had finished her song, Uncle Zechariah came in.

"Oh, Uncle Zechariah, how are you?" Mary said as she rushed to greet him.

He smiled kindly, but not a word did he say. Mary looked from him
to her Aunt Elizabeth,
whose face said,
"Wait a bit. I'll explain."

Just then Uncle Zechariah
went out again.

"I'll tell you the story, Mary," Aunt Elizabeth said, "but first, my dear, you must have a wash and something to eat. You must be hungry."

Later Aunt Elizabeth told Mary the story of Uncle Zechariah's duty in the Holy Place at the temple, that honor that only came once in a lifetime to a privileged priest, and to many priests never at all. She told how the angel Gabriel stood beside the altar and told Zechariah that his prayer for a baby was answered.

Aunt Elizabeth went on to tell Mary that Uncle Zechariah had not believed the angel, had actually argued a bit with Gabriel: "Can you believe it? These men! Said he wanted a sign. He got one. The angel said, 'A sign you will have, my friend. You will be dumb till the baby is born!' And Uncle Zechariah hasn't said a word since. Not one word!

"Poor man, it's awful to see him waving his arms about, trying to make folks understand him. Sometimes I wonder if he's deaf too. But you know, it serves him right. Fancy arguing with an angel! I don't think he'll do that again! He had to write me a note to give me the news. I was simply overjoyed. Of course, I don't need a note now!"

Aunt Elizabeth was a godly woman with a sense of humor.

"How good God is to me!" Aunt Elizabeth went on. "I'd always felt disgraced because I didn't have a family. Every Jewish woman hopes that her son will be Messiah, our Savior; so, no children, no hope. What an honor has fallen to you, Mary! And to me, for my son is to be Messiah's herald, the forerunner of the Savior."

Mary spent three months with Aunt Elizabeth, three happy months. How those two ladies talked, the one so young and the other so elderly. They laughed together for joy. And how they praised God!

In about a week's time now, Aunt Elizabeth's baby should arrive. Mary thought it was time she went home. In view of her own wedding preparations, still to be made, they had agreed that as soon as suitable fellow travelers could be found traveling north to or beyond Nazareth, Mary should go with them.

A family was heard of who were going north beyond Nazareth. They'd be pleased to have Mary travel with them. So Mary prepared to leave.

"I'm so glad you came, Mary," her Aunt Elizabeth said. "You've been such a cheerer-upper for me. You know, although I was really thrilled at the good news of the baby, at my age I was also a bit embarrassed. I'd hidden myself up for five months, till you came. What with me in hiding and Uncle Zechariah not speaking to me—how could he?—you really have been a joy to us.

God bless you on your homeward way, my dear! God has everything in hand, Mary."

Mary waved good-by to them from far down the road. And the dear old couple waved to her till she was out of sight.

Well, Elizabeth's baby finally arrived. It was a boy, of course, and the rejoicing was tremendous. All the neighbors came to congratulate Elizabeth and Zechariah. Any family members who were anywhere near were invited to the Ceremony to Name the Baby. (Mary and her family heard all about it in Nazareth, afterwards.)

It was some occasion, naming a baby—anytime. And since this was a miracle baby, being born to such elderly parents, there was more interest than usual in this naming ceremony. And poor Zechariah, the father, still could not speak.

Well, the baby was eight days old. A lovely little boy. Dressed like a little prince he was, lying in his cradle.

And the naming ceremony was to be on this very day.

There would be a party afterward, so all kinds of lovely food was prepared.

Elizabeth's friends had everything ready. Some of them were still adding finishing touches. Others hovered over the cradle, clucked their tongues and pinched the baby's face gently to get a smile from him—a smile at eight days old!

"Got a smile for auntie, darling? Dear little Zechariah!"

"Don't call him Zechariah!" Elizabeth said. "His name is John."

43

"What did you say, Elizabeth? Don't be ridiculous. Of course you'll call him Zechariah after his father. You can't call him John. There's no one in the family called John. That name doesn't mean a thing to us."

"John is the baby's name!" said Elizabeth decidedly. "He's God's gift."

Well, you know how some people are. Won't take no for an answer. They will go on and on. And they did. Since they couldn't make Elizabeth see sense, they started on Zechariah. They made gestures, waving their arms about. They treated the poor man as if he was deaf as a post, as well as dumb.

In self-protection, he gestured at them, showing that he wanted something to write on. Eventually, one of them got him a writing tablet. There was dead silence in the house as they craned their necks. Some had their mouths open, waiting to see what Zechariah—whose baby it was after all—would write.

"His name is JOHN," he wrote.

That did it! Before anyone could get in a word, Zechariah's voice was back, loud and clear. And he was praising God in a magnificent poem—beautiful thoughts that had been in his heart during the time that he could not speak. And you can read that poem in your Bible today. It's there!

Everybody—friends and neighbors and relations—everybody was filled with wonder, and a little awe.

The news of what had happened spread through the Judean hills. Everyone who heard said, "I wonder what this child is going to grow up to be."

They thought long about these happenings, turning them over in their minds. And they certainly had something to think about, especially the words of Zechariah's song.

"We'll hear more of that boy," they said. And they were right. There's a great story about him in the Bible—he became John the Baptist.

Meanwhile, Mary's journey home to Nazareth was uneventful enough. For the first part of the way, her mind was full of the conversations and happenings at her aunt's house. And it was a matter of walk, walk, walk, all day, on the dusty roads. Stops for meals and a sleep at night. As she got nearer home, though, the old

anxiety came back. She'd have to tell her mother and father the secret, and—and she'd have to tell Joseph.

Whatever would Joseph say? And mother? And father? Would they understand? God had told Aunt Elizabeth the secret Himself. Maybe, maybe God would tell them too. Aunt Elizabeth felt sure that God would tell them. Mary did hope so.

Had God told them? She'd know pretty soon now—as soon as she got home.

5

How Can I Tell Joseph?

Nazareth at last! It had been a long journey, but now Mary was nearly home. Half a mile or so still to walk, and she'd be home.

"I hope—I hope Joseph knows. I hope father and mother know too! Only God could have told them if they know. Only God can tell anybody my news—for them to really believe it. I could never tell anyone."

Mary knew well enough that people would have plenty to say about her having a baby before she was married—while she was just engaged to be married. Who'd believe that the baby was the Son of God and that it was God who was responsible for the baby?

She could imagine how some people would sneer and make nasty jokes. No, God would have to reveal it to those He wanted to tell.

But it was her fiancé, Joseph, she thought of most. What would Joseph say? Joseph would have the right to drop her, although it wouldn't be easy. In Israel an engagement was absolutely binding. The young couple didn't live together until the actual wedding, but by Jewish law they were legally bound by the engagement. Only a divorce could separate them. Joseph could divorce Mary.

So Mary faced divorce and disgrace and very severe punishment—as she walked up the hill in Nazareth on the very last lap of her journey home.

She shuddered.

Mary was the most honored girl of all time. But she could be the most misunderstood. Her secret made her heart almost burst for joy. But the way people would see it made Mary feel frightened and sick.

Walking up the hill, Mary thought of her engagement day and Joseph. Strong and trusting, reliable, so kind, was Joseph. She'd been proud that he'd chosen her, picked her out to be his bride. She'd always hoped he would.

Her parents and Joseph's parents had agreed to the engagement. Though, to her dad, was anybody worthy of his Mary? Now her parents would be shocked beyond words. It would kill her dad. They'd blame Joseph. And if he denied it and the elders of the synagogue believed him, which Mary was sure they would, she'd be treated as a wicked person, unfaithful, immoral, and—she'd be pushed over a cliff . . . and stoned to death . . . and left unburied for the jackels and the vultures to eat. She'd heard of women being stoned for immorality.

But what was it she'd said to the angel three months ago? "I am the Lord's, body and soul. Let all that you've said to me come true."

Yes, it was the angel's visit and what he'd said that made all the difference. "Shalom!" he'd said. "Mary, you are the most favored of all women, of all time. The most highly honored woman in the world, that ever was or will be. God has chosen you to be the mother of Messiah, God's Son, the promised Savior."

But Mary couldn't tell anyone that! God must tell them. No one would believe her. You can understand that, can't you?

"Mary's ho-ome!"
The children
of the household
welcomed
their sister.

The very young ones jumped around. They'd all missed her. Mary had a little gift for each of them, something small—"a wee minding," as my Scottish friends call it.

As her mother greeted her, Mary couldn't help but notice the anxious, questioning, almost suspicious look in her eyes. "Oh, dear, God hasn't told her." Mary knew He hadn't. "Please tell her, God—and daddy."

"Glad you're home, lass," her father said. "Had a nice holiday?" He was thankful to see his dear daughter home again.

There were so many things to talk about. And it wasn't long before Joseph came over. Mary, the traveler, was back. And they all *would* have her tell them all that had happened, as they sat round on the floor to listen.

50

Aunt Elizabeth and Uncle Zechariah were popular with the family. Mary had a real job answering the questions that were fired at her. However, when she started on the story of Aunt Elizabeth's baby—promised by the angel to Uncle Zechariah when he was the priest chosen to go into the holiest place on earth, the Holy Place in the temple, alone with God—everyone was quiet and listening.

. . . And because he didn't believe the angel's message, Uncle Zechariah was struck dumb. Hadn't said one single word all the time Mary had been there, nor for six months before that. He seemed to be deaf as well, Mary said. And he'd had to write a note to Aunt Elizabeth to tell her about the angel's promise: "God says you're—we're going to have a little boy, born to you, to be called John, who is the Messiah's herald.

Messiah will be on His way soon." That's what Uncle Zechariah had written on a clay tablet, a note for Aunt Elizabeth. "And maybe by now the baby will have arrived," Mary said as she finished telling about her visit.

The children had their eyes and their mouths wide open. Fancy Uncle Zechariah arguing with an angel! They did hope he would be able to speak again soon.

Joseph wanted to show Mary what he'd been doing, so he took her over to their little home-to-be. It was quite near her parents' home. "Why did you go away like that, Mary?" Joseph asked when they were alone. "Why did you?" Joseph had been sad about it. "All that time at your Aunt Elizabeth's— surely she didn't need you? She must have plenty of friends to help her." "I think she did need me, Joseph. For five months she'd stayed indoors out of sight, and Uncle Zechariah never speaking to her—he couldn't, poor man! She did need me, Joseph. I was able to cheer her up. But I'm home now, and I'm not going away again."

Mary turned her face away from him. She was worried that Joseph didn't know. None of them knew. "O God, do please tell them, especially Joseph."

Having got it off his chest that he was disappointed at her going away, Joseph was his old self again. Mary did love him. He was just the person to care for the Baby. But—but— what ever would he say?

Joseph had worked so hard while Mary was away. He must have been working all hours to have got so much done. The furniture was ready. The little house was fixed up.

"Joseph, you've finished it all already! You must have had no sleep."

"Very little while you were away. I've been anxious, Mary—You look different somehow . . . much more mature . . . grown up." ("O God, do tell him!" she prayed.)

Mary's heart ached as Joseph showed her all that he'd prepared for their little home. Maybe, after all, she would never share his dreams with him—if he decided to drop her.

She wouldn't be able to hide her secret for long now anyway. Everybody who saw her would know a baby was coming. People would talk. The fact would dawn on Joseph too, or he'd hear of it. Maybe God meant her to tell Joseph first—then God would explain to him. But how to tell him?

The man who was to be the foster father of Messiah must be a man of strong convictions, not just a man who could be touched by pity that might wear off. Joseph must be told without pleading looks, without coaxing tones of voice, without gestures. He must be told and left with the bare, bald statement. Then he'd be free to make up his mind.

Mary decided she would write him a note:

"Dear Joseph, I am going to have a baby. Maybe God will explain."

Mary gave the note to him the next evening. "Read this after you get home, Joseph," Mary said. Joseph read Mary's note:

"I am going to have a baby. Maybe God will explain."

"Maybe *what*? Maybe *God* will explain?"

6

Joseph's Dilemma

Joseph was horrified when he read Mary's note. His Mary, his beautiful, lovely, pure, faithful Mary was going to have a baby that wasn't his?

They weren't even married yet—only engaged to be married. Being engaged was binding enough, but of course they didn't live together—not yet. Not till their wedding, which would be in six months' time. It was getting late. Mary would have gone to bed in her parents' home by now. But then, in any case, explanations wouldn't help. Facts were facts. A baby was a fact. And its not being his was a fact. This would be an utter scandal very soon.

Mary would be in disgrace—and he, the upright, just Joseph, would be deeply involved, for Mary was his finacée.

What should he do? What should he say? Joseph was shaken to the depths of his being. Distraught. He paced about in the dark. Beads of perspiration stood on his brow. His nails cut into his hands as he clenched his fists. "Who's done this? O God, what has happened?"

For a long time Joseph paced back and forth. Then, weary and sad, he went to bed. As he lay there, broken-hearted and unable to sleep, he decided what he would do.

"If I say I don't know anything about this—which is true, I don't—the city elders will treat Mary as an immoral person and maybe have her . . . stoned to death . . . pushed over a cliff and stoned . . . left for the wild beasts and vultures to eat. No, I couldn't bear that." Joseph shuddered and broke into a cold sweat. Poor little Mary!—

"Or I could divorce her secretly, and Mary could go away by herself, and the baby could be born in seclusion somewhere. Then I would have nothing to do with her—or it.

"That would be the most merciful thing for me to do. It breaks my heart . . . but right is right . . . and justice is justice. I'd be being merciful, according to custom,

but—oh—" And Joseph sobbed a great deep sob from a broken heart.

Then he fell asleep in his grief. And while he slept he had a visitor. A bright, shining angel appeared and spoke to him.

"Joseph, descendant of David, don't be afraid to marry Mary your fiancée! That Baby she's going to have is God's Son, Messiah. Her Son is to be called Jesus, for He shall save His people from their sins. And you are to act as His father, and as His father you're to give Him His name."

Joseph woke up, thrilled and excited. God had chosen his wonderful Mary, his lovely fiancée, to be Messiah's mother! And God had chosen him, Joseph, carpenter of Nazareth, to be foster father to His Son, Messiah!

Joseph felt as chosen as Mary did. They were poor, but God had chosen them.

Joseph dressed quickly. Today he must bring Mary to the little home he'd prepared. What a good thing he'd finished it so early. He'd thought the wedding would be in six months' time, but the angel's message meant: *"Today.* And take very great care of her. She can be your wife proper after the baby is born."

And that's just what happened. Joseph got up early—very early—in the morning. "How worried poor Mary must be!" he said. "I suppose God must have told her about the baby, and she's never said anything to anybody. I wonder—oh, I must get to see her!"

At the very earliest moment that wouldn't seem too improper, Joseph was at Mary's parents' house.

"You there, Mary?" he called.

"Ah, that's Joseph's voice, and he sounds so happy!"

What a night Mary had had, wondering how Joseph would take the news. Would God explain to him? Now she knew God had told him—she knew by his cheerful voice.

"Now I can tell him about the angel telling me and

58

about Aunt Elizabeth knowing the news from God."

Mary did. Joseph was quite awe-struck by what Mary told him.

"And, Joseph, you're just as much God's honored one as I am."

"Yes, I know, Mary, and today you come home with me—God said so—to our little home. And I'll take care of you and the baby."

"How kind you are to me, Joseph. You're willing to bear reproach along with me. People will talk. You could have honorably cleared out of this responsibility," Mary said.

"People will talk some still. But they do have their own things to see and think about," Joseph said.

"You can see, Joseph, that I couldn't tell you. I'd have influenced you, and I'm sure we've got such a task ahead of us that we both need to be commissioned for the job. God had to speak to us each individually, separately."

Mary and Joseph praised God that He had chosen them to look after His Son's arrival on this earth. And the humble little home in Nazareth was ready for Him.

How Joseph worked! Every bit of wood he sawed off, every bit he planed, every nail he pounded in—he was working for the very Son of God.

There's much more of this story to come. And it's the most exciting story in the world.

7

Orders From Rome

In Rome, Caesar Augustus, the great emperor, was holding a meeting, a senate meeting, about—what do you think? *Money!*

There he was, with his Chancellor of the Exchequer, and his accountants, and all his financial experts. And Caesar Augustus was paying close attention to what his advisers were saying, for although he was the greatest, most powerful man on earth, Caesar Augustus listened to facts. He knew what to do with facts.

Caesar Augustus was *the* most powerful man on earth—rich too, very rich.

He'd been called to power when he was still a student—only eighteen. There he'd been, quietly pursuing his studies, when the summons came.

"Octavian"—that was his name—"Octavian, you must go to Rome at once! Your Uncle Julius has been murdered, and in his will he named you as his heir."

"Uncle Julius murdered? Uncle Julius Caesar *murdered*? How come?" Octavian was shocked. Uncle Julius was closer to Octavian than just an uncle. Octavian's mother was Julius Caesar's niece, sure enough, but Uncle Julius Caesar had legally adopted Octavian and called him his very own son.

"Uncle Julius, my father, dead? Murdered?"

"To Rome at once, Octavian!" the summons said.

Octavian rolled up his study parchments, packed quickly, and set out for Rome.

As he traveled, he figured that he'd have rivals in Rome—rivals for power. Yes, there'd be Mark Antony and Lepidus. They'd be his rivals. And there'd be others.

As Octavian came into Rome that day, he saw it with new eyes. It was a city of brick—he would beautify it. And through the years he did. He turned it into a city of marble. He beautified the streets, planted trees and gardens. He had great viaducts and aqueducts built. Octavian brought the wealth of conquered lands into Rome—but that was through the years.

Right now, as Octavian came into Rome, a youth of eighteen, he had rivals. But he was the popular choice of the people, Caesar's heir. The veteran army rallied to his support, and Octavian forced his main rivals, Mark Antony and Lepidus, to come to terms with him.

A triumvirate was set up—a government of three— Octavian himself, Mark Antony, and Lepidus. It was a powerful triumvirate. It smashed up the forces of Brutus, one of the men who had killed Octavian's uncle, and put down uprisings of any kind. The triumvirate, the three rulers, divided the widespread Roman dominions among themselves.

Lepidus was soon stripped of his power. So Octavian and Mark Antony were left to share control of the world—the known world. Antony had control of the eastern countries, while Octavian controlled Italy and the west.

Antony didn't pay attention to his part of the empire. He fell in love with Cleopatra, the queen of Egypt, and dallied around her court for more than a year. Octavian seized this opportunity to make himself sole master of the world.

Cleopatra, queen of Egypt, was an arrogant woman. Octavian decided to declare war on her—and thus on Antony. Octavian's fleet won a decisive victory off the coast of Greece. Antony and Cleopatra were alarmed. And when they heard that Octavian's fleet was sailing toward Egypt, they panicked and committed suicide.

Octavian was now master of the world, the first Roman emperor, master of the great Roman Empire.

He was acclaimed *the Caesar.* His Roman senate thought so much of him that they gave him the name *Augustus*—meaning "majestic"—*Caesar Augustus.* (People actually began to worship him!) His friends Virgil and Horace wrote poetry about him—and about Rome.

Now, even the great deified Caesar Augustus couldn't be everywhere at once, and travel in those days was slow and very difficult. So he appointed kings or rulers to govern the countries that he'd conquered. Julius Caesar, his uncle (adopted father), had done the same thing before him.

Right now, at the time our story took place, Herod was the appointed king in Judea in Israel. (Israel was part of Caesar Augustus's empire.) Yes, Herod was king of the Jews at this time, under Emperor Caesar Augustus.

Well, Caesar Augustus was holding a senate meeting in Rome, discussing—you know what—*money!* Let's get back to that meeting.

There was Caesar Augustus with his Chancellor of the Exchequer, his accountants—in fact, with all the money men of Rome.

A wise man was speaking: "Peace cannot be secured or maintained without armies; and armies cannot exist without pay; and payment cannot exist without taxation."

"We have peace throughout the whole world for the first time in—let me see—two hundred years," Caesar said. "Today we can shut the doors of Janus's temple. Never for two hundred years have the doors of Janus's temple been shut. (The doors of Janus's temple were only shut when there was peace all over the world.) People rejoice in Pax Romana, the peace that Rome has given to the world. But I know well enough the need of a strong, powerful army to keep the peace," Caesar said.

"Yes, your Majesty, there could be revolts—uprisings among the Jews in Judea, for instance."

"Herod's in charge there. He has his own way of doing things," Caesar replied. "Strange fellow! Very cruel. But loyal to me here in Rome. Very loyal. He built that magnificent seaport Caesarea for me—named it after me, too. I understand the Jews don't like it. And Herod has his problems managing them.

"But I can't understand why more money doesn't come in to Rome. We need it—the aqueducts, viaducts, roads, the civil service, and the huge cost of keeping a big army all over the place. I still can't understand how the tribute money of all these countries we've conquered can possibly be so small. We need money. We must get more money. But how?"

"If I may say so," a shrewd little senator spoke up, "how can your Majesty know how much tax to levy, or how much money to expect when the tax is levied, unless your Majesty knows the precise number of your Majesty's subjects and how much property they own?"

"Well-spoken, senator! We must take another count. We'll take another census in each country. Every man, every woman, shall be counted, along with their property and their children," Caesar Augustus said.

"Each of my rulers knows his own nation. Each king or ruler will take the count, the census, as he can best carry it out."

So the whole world was to be counted—to make sure they paid their full tax to Caesar Augustus.

And the news came to Israel: "Caesar Augustus has decreed that a census is to be taken."

Herod relayed the message to the Jews, having decided that the winter solstice was the time for it. (That was the time around the shortest day of the year, about December 22.) And the best way for the Jews to be counted was for them to report to the census takers in the city of their ancestors, he decided. Some people hadn't left their ancestral city, but others had. In fact, quite a lot had.

"Each Jew is to return to the city of his ancestors and report there."

Caesar Augustus in Rome may never ever have heard of Nazareth—probably he hadn't. But his notice went up in the marketplace in Nazareth:

At the winter solstice every one of you is to go to the city of your ancestors to be counted for tax purposes.
Decree made by Emperor Caesar Augustus.

Signed: King Herod

Joseph was in the marketplace in Nazareth that morning, loading his little donkey with supplies of wood that he'd just bought for his work in his carpenter's shop. He was busy trying to arrange the wood on the donkey's back, but he could hear angry voices, and as he looked up for a minute across the marketplace he could see people gathered round the news board.

A man he knew—he knew most people in Nazareth—was coming towards him right now.

"Seen the notice, Joseph? We've all gotta be taxed—counted first—in our hometown. Decree from the emperor. That's a downright nuisance. I can't afford to be away from my work for a couple of weeks to report to my hometown. Dear, oh dear! It's going to hit you too. Where'll you have to go? Oh, yes, you're Bethlehem, line of David, I remember.

"It isn't fair, being ruled by these foreigners from Rome. Tax! Tax! Tax! I suppose they're really gonna make us pay this time. And it's signed 'King Herod.' *He's* not our king. Wish we had our own ruler. This Herod, he's anybody's body—except ours. Knows

70

which side his bread's buttered with the emperor. Oh, why doesn't our Messiah come?"

Joseph could have told this man quite a story, couldn't he? But he and his wife, Mary, knew that only God could reveal His Son to people.

Joseph went to look at the notice, leading his little loaded donkey.

Now this was really the most awkward thing. He had a number of orders that simply had to be finished. People getting married relied on Joseph to get their furniture made. Several beds and tables and chests simply had to be done before the winter solstice. And several little homes were waiting to be fixed up for young people who would be newlyweds by the winter solstice.

Well, Joseph supposed that long hours and hard work would get *them* finished. But—but what could he do about Mary? That was just the very time that her baby was to arrive. He couldn't leave her in Nazareth while he trudged off to Bethlehem, ninety miles away.

As he passed along the street, two men were talking together.

"Women got to go too, this time; cripples, everybody. This has got to be a very accurate count. Caesar Augustus needs money, and we gotta pay up. Nobody left

out either. They do just what they like with us. We need our own ruler. Herod's no friend of Israel—toadies to Rome all the time. I gotta go trailing to—"

Joseph asked at the information center.

"Nobody is excused, sir, from this counting. I'm afraid, sir, you must just make your way to your native city. Which is it?"

"Bethlehem."

"It's a long way—ninety miles, I guess—but I can't help it. Sorry, sir. We just have to take orders from the top and pass them on. Don't blame me."

Joseph was troubled. He walked with his little donkey on up the hill. He was right into his carpenter's shop before he noticed where he was.

His house joined his carpenter's shop, and the clatter of the donkey's hoofs had brought Mary to the door of their little home.

"Oh, Joseph," she said, "you've been longer than you said."

"Yes, Mary, and I've got bad news for you. Gotta go to Bethlehem."

"Bethlehem! When? Whatever for?"

8

Gotta Go to Bethlehem

Why would Joseph have to go to Bethlehem now, Mary wondered.

"Decree from Caesar about the taxing. Everybody's got to go to their own city to be counted. And ours is Bethlehem, ninety miles away—and at the winter solstice. There's a notice in the marketplace. Everybody is talking about it, standing around and saying it isn't fair. Some are saying, 'Why can't we have our Messiah, instead of being ruled by Rome?' "

"The winter solstice did you say, Joseph? That's just when the baby is to be born! Oh, Joseph, I shall miss you. What shall I do without you?"

"No, Mary, you've got to go too."

"Me?"

"Yes, You've got to go too, Mary. It does worry me. It's not safe for you to travel all that way."

"But Joseph, Joseph—can't you see what's happened? The emperor in Rome doesn't even know us, and he's made a law that we're to go to Bethlehem, and the baby will be born in Bethlehem, as the prophet foretold in the Scripture. *We'd* never have thought of going to Bethlehem! Now we're being made to go!

I had wondered sometimes how the Scripture was going to be fulfilled—about Messiah being born in Bethlehem. I couldn't figure that bit out. Oh, Joseph!—"

"But, my dear, that very long journey. Is it safe for you?"

"Of course it is safe. The baby is the Son of God—Messiah. God, His Father, will surely take care of Him—and us."

Joseph began to unload the donkey.

"Well, little donkey," he said, "you'll be coming too —on the long journey." And he patted the little beast. The donkey tossed his head and twitched his ears as if he understood.

Mary's heart sang for joy. Already she'd begun to think of what things she'd need to get ready for the journey to Bethlehem. She must take the baby clothes anyway.

"Just as we head for Bethlehem, other people will head for Nazareth, I suppose, and other towns. What a lot of traveling!" Mary said.

"There'll be a lot of people who won't go anywhere," Joseph said. "People who've never moved from where they were born."

But all over the known world, the Roman Empire, people prepared for journeys—in Spain and Germany and Italy and France and Egypt—and I guess our ancestors in Britain who lived south of Hadrian's Wall had to go to be taxed then, too. England was part of the Roman Empire. And many of us who speak English today, whether with an American accent or Australian or whatever, and those of us who speak French and German and Spanish and Hebrew and Arabic—we, most of us, had ancestors who had to be counted in Caesar Augustus's census. Whether they had to make a journey to a distant town for it, or to one near at hand, or whether they just stayed where they'd been born, counted they had to be when Caesar Augustus made his decree from Rome.

So there were comings and goings all over the world!

But our spotlight is really on the two from Nazareth—Mary and Joseph—as they set out, heading south for Bethlehem, to be counted. Nazareth to Bethlehem was a five days' journey.

Their little donkey had an assortment of bundles attached to his harness. A skin flagon of water was a must, and some food for the journey—bread, nuts, raisins, some dried meat and fish (some corn for the donkey himself, though he could eat grass along the way).

Some of Joseph's tools had to go—just had to—some of the smaller ones. Joseph wouldn't think of not having a few of his tools with him, any more than I'd think of going anywhere without my needlepoint and pens and notebook and camera and recorder and—oh, where am I going to stop? You always take things with you on a journey, don't you? We all have to have our baggage with us, our bits and pieces.

Joseph had a hammer, and a few nails, and a chisel, and a knife for wood carving—maybe even a plane. Mary had oil and clothes for the baby, long strips of cloth to wrap Him up in, so that He would grow tall and straight. She had all that she needed in her bundle. She'd been taught to look after newborn babies. All the girls learned how to do that.

Mary rode on the donkey's back some of the way, though she was glad to walk beside Joseph sometimes. You can have too much of donkey riding—all day for five days.

At night they could sleep at somebody's house or at inns—sometimes. Everybody seemed to be traveling, so there wasn't much inside accommodation at inns. Accommodation was at a premium—first come, first served. You had to be important and rich to send a messenger ahead to book accommodation in advance. Mary and Joseph could sleep in the open, of course, under the stars in a sheltered spot. But it could be cold at night, though the days were warm. And the roads were dusty. Unpaved roads are very dusty anywhere in the world if the weather is dry. They are muddy and slippery if the weather is wet.

Mary and Joseph were on the greatest adventure with God that ever was. In many ways, the whole thing was God's great secret. But God had elected to tell the secret to a few selected people—we shall hear more of that later.

Mary and Joseph were right in the middle of God's secret. They, of course, didn't talk about it to anyone.

God had chosen Mary to be the mother of His Son—Messiah. Mary was the most highly favored woman of all time. Gabriel, the archangel sent to her from God, had told her so. And, of course, he'd told her about the baby.

But Mary was just a humble girl, and that's the bit that onlookers knew—a poor humble girl married to a young village carpenter who'd just set up in business on his own. And the gossips said that her baby shouldn't be arriving so soon. They were rather surprised at Joseph—quiet, sensible fellow he'd seemed to be.

Of course, the gossips couldn't know that God had sent His angel to tell Joseph that *he* was chosen to be Messiah's guardian. He was the man who was to act as Messiah's father, give him His name, provide for His food and clothes, and train Him as He grew up. Imagine the honor Joseph had!

Mary and Joseph and God.

But the people in the town couldn't possibly know that, unless God told them. And He didn't, so they didn't know. They judged by outward appearances, which at any time can be very misleading.

Mary had heard all kinds of old wives' tales that went round Nazareth. Always she'd said to herself: "But the baby is the Son of God. I don't need to pay attention to old superstitions." And she hadn't.

At the village well, as the women drew the water up in the bucket attached to the long strong rope and poured it splashing into the stone jars they'd brought from home, advice poured out to Mary when it was known that she had to go to Bethlehem, ninety miles away. Most of the women had never been so far in their lives—to Jerusalem, yes, to the temple, but Bethlehem was farther still.

"What mother-to-be sets off on a ninety-mile walk, even riding on a donkey part of the way, a ninety-mile journey just before her baby is due to be born?" they murmured.

Mary and Joseph were well on their journey now. Many times as they'd traveled, Joseph had said, "Mary, m'dear, are you all right? I do hope the baby won't be born until we're settled in comfortable quarters in Bethlehem."

"Joseph, I'm fine. This is what has been decreed—our journey to Bethlehem. The emperor has decreed it. It's inevitable. You can't do anything about that, so don't worry. You can't change it.

"And don't worry about me. I'm quite all right. All this walking is the best thing in the world. If I was at home, I guess I'd be scrubbing and cleaning the house. Quite often mothers-to-be get a burst of energy just before the baby is due to arrive. I'm quite all right. And Messiah has to be born in Bethlehem, the Scripture says so; we'll get there all right. God has everything in hand."

"But I just feel responsible for looking after you better than this, Mary."

"Joseph, God is in charge of this operation. We'll get our guidance from Him if we listen. Really, as you think about it, there's nothing—simply nothing—that we *can* do about it. It's all arranged for us."

"You're right, Mary! We must just trust God. But I do *want* to help you all I can."

"You're the dearest, kindest man on earth, Joseph, one of God's gentlemen. *The* one of God's gentlemen. We're in God's hands. I'm going to enjoy every bit of the journey that I can. It's God's plan, not ours. He'll look after us."

The journey was long, of course—five days. There were many travelers to and from the north, all making their way to their native cities to be counted.

Mary and Joseph didn't have far to go now. They'd reached Jerusalem, the golden, walled city on the hill. The white-walled, rebuilt temple seen above the walls of the city, gleamed in the sunshine in spite of a pall of blue smoke that hung over the spot where the sacrifice fires smoldered. The smell of the sacrifices made the travelers hungry. It smelled like a giant-sized cookout. They'd heard the sound of the silver trumpets on the wind earlier in the day as they'd traveled.

"Just a few more miles now, Mary, and we'll be there," Joseph said.

They were passing the spot where Rachel had died the day Benjamin was born. Joseph shuddered as he saw the grave.

"No gloomy thoughts now, Joseph," Mary said. "God is taking care of His Messiah, and He is taking care of you and me."

"All the same, I'll be glad when we arrive in Bethlehem."

On they went. It was getting dusk now. The stars had begun to peep out in the sky. Joseph had to watch his steps all the time, for the road was stony, and the donkey was quite heavily laden. Mary was riding now.

"Joseph, look at that beautiful star! I've never seen such a big, bright star in my life!"

There was Bethlehem. The lights had begun to twinkle. The road was still quite crowded with travelers heading for the town.

Joseph led the donkey up the winding road. Away to the left lay the hills where David had kept his father's sheep long ago. Even now shepherds were over there and in the valley below the road. You could hear them whistling and calling to each other in the dark.

Ah, there was the inn. You couldn't miss it. Crowds of people were there in the courtyard. Lanterns hung on the outer walls, and everywhere there were camels and donkeys and people.

"At last we're here," Joseph said. "And all's well. The inn looks busy, but—now for a comfortable bed and a good night's sleep."

"Joseph—I think—I think—the baby might come—tonight."

"Do you? Let me quickly ask the innkeeper for a room!"

86

9

A Baby! On a Night Like This!

The inn at Bethlehem was crowded. Everybody belonging to King David's line, every one of King David's descendants, had come to Bethlehem for the census-taking.

The inn rooms built round the courtyard were full. They'd been reserved early. Messengers had been sent on ahead to book accommodation for important people. Hillel, the great and famous rabbi, had been booked in early with his family. They were probably already asleep by now, comfortable in the best accommodation that the inn could offer.

At the end of their ninety-mile journey from Nazareth, Joseph and Mary were faced with a sign: "NO VACANCIES."

"No room in here, buddy," someone yelled as Joseph arrived at the courtyard entrance, leading the donkey with Mary on its back.

Normally, as an overnight traveler you could easily get a room. You could tether your donkey or camel outside your room, and the innkeeper would sell you food.

But tonight the courtyard was crammed with weary people, donkeys, and camels all mixed up together.

People were complaining, joking, laughing loudly, and passing remarks, as people will do, as they sat and lolled and ate their suppers on the ground. Mary and Joseph could smell garlic and stews. The lanterns standing about and hanging on the walls threw wavering light on all kinds of faces.

"I'll just be a minute," Joseph told Mary. "I must get us a place to stay quickly. I'll go and ask the innkeeper for some place, somewhere. Keep your eyes on me and the lantern. I won't be out of your sight. That looks like the main door over there where there are more lanterns hanging around. I'll find him anyway. You'll be all right for a minute, won't you?"

Joseph had begun to pick his way through the squatting people to find the innkeeper.

He didn't wait to answer the man squatting on the ground eating his supper who said, "It's no good going there, buddy. You'll just have to bed down out here like the rest of us. You can get somethin' to eat from the innkeeper, if you haven't brought anything with ya. But I should think his supplies is running pretty short by now."

But just then Mary, waiting on the donkey's back, noticed bakers' boys carrying in large baskets of piping hot bread on their heads. Mary could smell the delicious fresh bread. The bakers were cashing in on the crowds.

Joseph banged on the inn door. The innkeeper opened it.

"Have you got a room for two from the Galilee, please?"

The innkeeper threw up his arms in dismay. Then, with a sweep of his right arm, told Joseph, "Look at the crowd out there, all wanting rooms."

"But—but—but—," Joseph stammered, "the baby may be born this very night. Isn't there a little private spot somewhere? It doesn't have to be fancy, though I'd like the best I could possibly get for her —and the baby."

"A *baby!* On a night like this, with all this crowd of people about! Huh, huh, huh, goodness gracious me! All I've got is one of the stables at the back. I believe there's one at the end there pretty clean. That's all I've got, young fella. I'm sorry, but that's all. You're just lucky I didn't think of the stable earlier for some of them others. Plenty of 'em would be glad of that stable 'stead of being out all night. Hope it doesn't rain on 'em or snow. This is a mess, this census, and no mistake. Rome telling us what to do. I wish our Messiah would come and put an end to all this ruling from Rome. Here, take this lantern and go round behind the inn."

"I've got a lantern," Joseph said.

"Well, it won't hurt for you to have two. When you see where you gotta go, you'll be glad of two. You can fix the place up as you want. The animals won't hurt you. Make a little fire outside, if that'll help you."

"Can you give us hot water and some food?"

"Sure, friend, at a small cost."

"Oh, of course," Joseph said. "I expect to pay."

"You can heat water on your little fire when you make it down there. Where's your wife?"

"Over there by the courtyard entrance, with the donkey."

Just then more people arrived, and the innkeeper was called off in another direction.

With an anxious heart Joseph turned back to Mary.

"I'm so sorry, dear. They're absolutely full up. I could even see people sleeping on the floor inside when he opened the door. But he told me we could have a stable all to ourselves at the back, if we like. Just a few animals in it. And I can light a fire outside somewhere at the back. I'm so sorry, Mary, that there's nothing better."

"We'll manage, Joseph. You know who's in charge of this operation, don't you? And if God has planned it so, who are we to complain?"

"You're a great girl, Mary! You're right. It's only that I feel I've let you down, just when you needed something good."

"With all these people about, it will be far better to have the stable to ourselves. A stable with God is quite all right. Let's get to it!"

10

Born in a Stable

Mary and Joseph picked their way through the noisy crowd in the courtyard. And anybody looking must have been surprised to see a girl, a fellow, and a donkey disappear round the side of the inn.

The path, lighted by the lanterns Joseph carried, led them to the stable, which was a cave, a natural cave, hewn a bit out of the rock. It was as private as could be.

There were a few sleeping animals that stirred a little when they discovered they were having company. They opened their sleepy eyes for a moment; the lights made them blink. Some sheep stood up, a couple of hens clucked. The donkeys seemed excited to see another donkey arrive.

Joseph hung one lantern on a nail in the wall. There was a heap of fresh hay over in the corner of the comfy cave, and beside it a heap of barley straw. In the solid limestone rock that was the back wall of the cave, about three feet up from the floor, was a recess, hewn out to make a manger, a feeding trough for the animals. The floor of the recess had been scooped out a bit to hold the hay and the corn. A block of salt usually lay at the bottom of mangers—animals love a lick of salt! There were other mangers hewn out at varying heights along the back wall of the cave.

The cave was a private, cozy shelter from the cold night. If Mary and Joseph had had time to listen they'd have heard the dim noise of the crowded courtyard, behind and above them. They would have heard a couple of shepherds whistling and calling to each other in the valley below them, and the odd bleat of a restless sheep. And through the cave doorway they'd have seen the outline of the Judean hills against the starlit sky.

But they were far too busy to look or listen.

Joseph had already cleared a space on the floor near the manger with a reed brush he'd found leaning against the wall. Now he was putting down fresh, clean straw and hay to make a comfortable bed for Mary.

Mary had taken off her traveling cloak and brushed out her long hair, while their little donkey had a drink of water from the drinking trough that stood near the cave

entrance. He was soon holding a donkey conversation with the other donkeys in the stable. Mary had taken her precious bundle off his back.

The baby's clothes were in that bundle—and oils, and just everything that a mother needed for a new baby in those days (which wasn't very much, compared with today).

It didn't take Joseph long to fix up a comfortable resting place. And with pieces of wood he found lying about in the cave and his tools (good thing he'd brought them!), he was able to fix up a most private little enclosure for Mary. The hay and the straw had a sweet smell, and the dried flowers in the hay reminded them of springtime in the meadows.

Joseph finished unloading the donkey and helped Mary wash her tired feet with water from the animals' drinking trough.

"I'd like you to get some warm water, Joseph—hot water. We'll need it. And bring down some nice hot bread from the inn. Baskets of it were arriving when we came in."

So Joseph went out. Mary had wanted him out of the way. It wouldn't be proper for him to be there when the baby was arriving—not like now when daddies can stay while the baby is born.

Mary felt sure that the baby was coming. And He did.

It was a beautiful birth, the birth of the Son of God. God saw to it that it was. Mary had no one to help her. She didn't need anyone to help her. She had God. And she had tremendous joy in her heart, and love, and great energy, and no fear in her mind.

The baby arrived so quickly. He gave a little cry, as newborn babies do—to let you know they're here! It's their "Hi! Hello!" And Mary knew exactly what to do with a new baby. Girls then were taught what to do—and now God helped her do it.

I can't describe to you the joy that flooded Mary's heart when she looked at her darling baby, who was the Son of God, the Messiah. No, I just can't tell you. But I can imagine she said, "Oh, you dear little boy! I must give you a kiss. I'm so glad you've come." (That's what I said to my little boy when he arrived.)

As Mary took the baby in her arms she was looking into the face of the Son of God, the Messiah. Her heart nearly burst for joy. I told you she knew how to look after Him. She'd brought oil for His little body, and she'd brought yards of soft white cloth to wrap Him in so that He'd grow straight and tall.

Mary had some soft cloth left after she'd wrapped Him. She laid the spare cloth on top of the clean hay in the cozy recess that was the manger. You could call this manger a hole in the wall, but it was the coziest place for a newborn baby's bed on a cold winter night.

Then Mary rested on the soft hay bed that Joseph had got ready for her.

Joseph could come back now as soon as he liked. Mary waited for him to come back with the bread. She was hungry!

11

Have You Seen Him?

Joseph was on his way back to the cave. Mary could hear his footsteps. He'd been away quite a while.

Almost before he was at the doorway, he called, "Mary, m'dear, are you all right? I'm sorry I've been away so long. Such a job I had with the fire, collecting kindling and something to burn—in the dark—and the line-up for the bread! You never saw anything like it. But I was lucky. I got some. They all didn't. And, at last, I've got some hot water for you—

"Oh, Mary!—what's happened?"

Mary was sitting up on the hay bed he'd made for her, leaning her back against the wall of the cave. Her face was radiant, angelic.

Mary just pointed to the manger—the rock recess in the wall beside her.

Joseph looked. Went closer. Peered into the hay. "Messiah! Son of God!" he cried as he saw the little sleeping baby. And Joseph, clutching a jar of hot water in one hand and some hot rolls of bread in the other, fell on his knees and worshiped Messiah, who was the baby, God's Son.

Then Joseph gave Mary a most loving kiss.

Mary was hungry. She enjoyed the delicious fresh bread Joseph had brought. Joseph enjoyed it too.

They were too happy to talk for a while. Joseph sat beside Mary on the bed of straw, holding her hand.

Then he said, "Well, well! Here we are in a cave on a hillside. Tonight the Son of God has come—the Messiah—right here. But who—who will ever believe it?

"They're waiting for Messiah all over Israel. Hillel the great Pharisee and his son Simeon look for Messiah all the time. They're sleeping in the inn above us now. Will they know that Messiah is born under their very noses? I wonder, will anybody know?"

Just then there was a noise outside the entrance to the cave—excited, muffled voices—people falling over each other it sounded like. And queer shadows appeared on the cave walls, cast by lanterns bobbing up and down.

Mary was startled. "Don't you worry, Mary m'dear," Joseph said, giving her hand a tight squeeze. "I'll deal with it." And in two or three strides Joseph was outside the cave to investigate and see what the ruckus was all about.

Mary listened intently. Excited men's voices. Rough, uncultured voices. Their accent was not the same as Galilee's, and they *would* all talk at once. But one voice was a bit clearer than the rest. Mary trained her ear on it.

"We've looked and searched everywhere for Him *(Who've they lost?* Mary wondered) in all the stables we could find. We've woke no end of people up lookin'

for Him. Some of 'em snorted at us and told us to 'get lost.' Suppose it was late, but we forgot the time. We was so excited. The angel said, 'Go and look! Find Him.' And we've looked everywhere. We saw a light here. Is He here, sir?"

Mary could imagine Joseph peering into their faces in the lantern light.

"Who are you?" he asked. "Where've you come from?"

"We're shepherds, come out of the fields—we've left our sheep out there. We've looked everywhere for Him. Where is He? We wish we could find Him."

"Now could just one of you explain? And please tell me what it is you've lost."

"You tell him, Rue."

"No, no, you're better at recountin' than I am, Pete," Rue said. "I'll help you if you get stuck."

So Pete told the story.

"Well, we're looking for a new baby. Do you know where He is? He's the promised Messiah, the angel said. (Mary was listening carefully now!) And the angel said He'd be lying in a manger, wrapped in swaddling clothes.

"We've looked everywhere, in all the stables in Bethlehem, round about, but we haven't found Him.

"You see, it was like this. We should have been settled down for the night, but our sheep was restless. The goats too, funny animals. Then an angel stood among us and spoke to us.

"At first, we thought it was some magic trick— somebody come to blind us and steal our sheep. But no, it wasn't. There stood a shining angel. We blinked. We was terrified. I went flat on the ground. But he said, 'Don't be afraid,' ever so kind like. So I looked up a bit.

104

"'To you', he said —he was looking straight at me—'to you a Savior is born this very day in David's city. The Savior, Christ the Lord.' That's Messiah, isn't it? Them was his very words, 'A Savior, Christ the Lord, born to you and all people, today'—his very words.

"There we all was, shielding our eyes from the bright shinin' light, and then—oh—there was music, beautiful music, strains of it, catchin' you, liftin' you up nearly into heaven. Oh, it was so beautiful! I'll never forget it. There were ever so many angels then in the sky, praisin' God and sayin', 'Glory to God in the highest and on earth peace, good will toward men'—their very words.

"It was as if the heavens opened and we saw all them angels. Then it all faded. We was on our faces again by this time.

"Then, you know what it's like when you've seen something like that—you wonder if you've imagined it. We said to each other, 'Did you see what I saw? Did you hear what I heard?'

"Of course, we all did. We thought over what we saw and heard: 'To you is born today in the City of David'— that's Bethlehem, for sure . . . 'a Savior who is Christ the Lord'—that's Messiah, isn't it? . . . 'You'll find the babe wrapped in swaddling clothes and lying in a manger.' A manger—why did he say (the angel), 'You'll *find* the baby and His mother'? He must have meant us to go and look. So we're lookin' in stables, because that's where you find mangers.

"We've asked everybody, as I told you. We've woke people up. They've swore at us. But we're still looking for the baby. Fancy God telling *us* —shepherds!"

By this time, Mary, listening inside, was thrilled and praising God in her heart. God had told them!

Joseph was standing outside with the shepherds, really guarding the entrance to the cave. He was awe-struck, speechless. It was a dark night now, but the flickering flames of the shepherds' lanterns did make a pool of light around them.

The shepherd spokesman, Pete, was still talking. "Do you happen to know where the baby and His mother are? If so, do tell us. Please tell us."

"He's here. Must just have been born at the very time the angel told you," Joseph said.

The shepherds surged forward to enter the cave. "At last! At last! We've found—" Then they stopped.

"Is it too soon? Will His mother allow us? Will you allow us?"

"One minute," Joseph said. He went inside to ask Mary. Mary just nodded with one of her beautiful smiles. And in came the rough shepherds.

Now it would have been improper, according to custom in those days, for them to speak to Mary. But she'd heard every word they'd spoken to Joseph. She just had to smile a welcome to them.

The reverence of those shepherds! On tiptoe they followed Joseph over to the manger. There they stood round the manger, gazing with wonder at the baby

whose little body was wrapped in swaddling clothes, as the angel had said.

One by one they set down their flickering lanterns on the floor, fell on their knees, and worshiped the baby, the Son of God.

The moments turned into minutes.

Mary watched the faces of the shepherds as they bowed in reverent worship. Their lanterns had brought added light into the cave. Some were just shepherd boys, like David had been years before. Some were weather-beaten men. They all worshiped. Here and there Mary saw a rough hand brush a glistening tear away.

These were holy, sacred moments, and Mary stored the memory of them away in her heart. She stored them away along with the other marvelous memories associated with the birth of her wonderful Son, God's Son.

One by one the shepherds stirred, rose from their knees, picked up their lanterns, and went out into the night, filled with wonder and joy. Mary smiled good-by to them. She looked radiant and angelic herself.

The shepherds waited for each other outside the cave, and Joseph went out to see them off.

They began to talk again. Pete, the spokesman, said: "And to think that God sent His Messiah, His Son, to a home just like ours. We live in a cave over on that hill. We sleep on straw. I'm glad Messiah was born in a place like mine. I've always heard He was coming in great glory. If He had, He'd have been out of the reach of the likes of me—us."

"Yes, we're glad, we're glad!" And off they went, praising God.

For days they told everybody. Even to their dying day, it was the first thing they said to people they met. Angels had brought the news of Messiah's birth to them. And they'd seen the baby Messiah.

But who'd believe *them?* They were only shepherds. Who'd ever believe anything a shepherd said?

What a day it had been! At last the little family slept—Mary and Joseph and the baby.

Mary and Joseph had come to Bethlehem to be counted. Now there was one more to add to the list—tomorrow.

And God had begun to tell more people about His Son.

For more stories about Mary and Joseph and the baby Jesus, look for *Come, Meet Jesus, the Boy.*